Life of Fred®

Ducks

Stanley F. Schmidt, Ph.D.

Polka Dot Publishing

ISBN: 978-1-937032-28-9
Printed and bound in the United States of America
Polka Dot Publishing   Reno, Nevada

To order books in the Life of Fred series,

visit our website PolkaDotPublishing.com

Questions or comments? Email the author at lifeoffred@yahoo.com

First Printing
This book was illustrated by the author with additional clip art furnished under license from Nova Development Corporation, which holds the copyright to that art.

Dear Parent,

Kids want to learn about the world, and they want to have fun. The Eden Series does both.

In this book we count to three on two occasions.

We do a little geometry: a square.

We illustrate three emotions: sad, happy, and afraid. (In some psychology books they list four emotions: glad, sad, mad, and afraid. ← They almost rhyme!)

They read a letter—complete with opening and closing salutations and a pink duck.

And there's a picture of me with my sticker collection.

Stan

Chapter One

"Duck"
by Fred

Kingie shouted, "Stop!"

"You made three mistakes."

Mistake number 1:

"Your duck
has two mouths."

"Duck"
by Fred

Mistake number 2:

"Duck"
by Fred

Kingie said, "The feet are wrong. They should be like this."

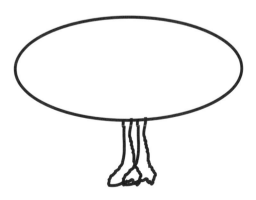

Mistake number 3:

Kingie asked, "Why do you draw square heads?

"Duck"
by Fred

This is a square.

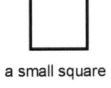

a small square

a pink square

THIS IS SQUARE WRITING.

This is pink writing.

This is fat writing.

This is handwriting.

"Duck"
by Kingie

Kingie painted a
picture of a duck.

Chapter Two

Duck Food

I did!

happy Kingie

Many people feed ducks old bread.

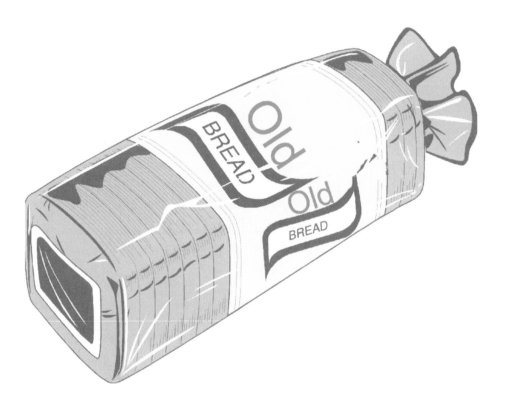

Ducks really like Duck Food.

One duck phoned his friends.

They got real Duck Food!

All the ducks came.

STOP!

you shout.

You made three mistakes in this picture.

There are 8 ducks in this picture.

Mistake number 1:

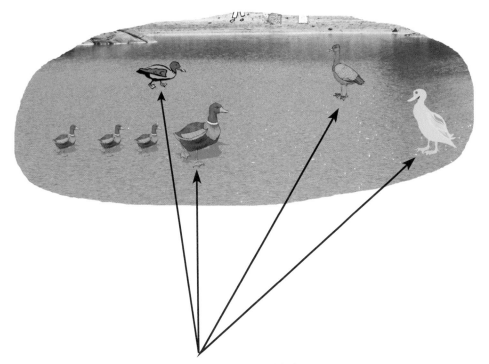

The ducks are walking
on the water!
They should be swimming.

Mistake number 2:

That duck is smiling!
It has two mouths.

Mistake number 3:

That duck is pink!

A letter to my readers . . .

Dear Readers,

My name is Stan. I wrote *Life of Fred:*

Ducks.   This is me.

I started with this duck.

I wanted to make him happy.

So I drew a smile.

You tell me that it is a mistake to draw

a pink duck.

Would you like a yellow and green duck

filled with apples?

When you write a book, you can draw

anything you like.

Your friend,

Stan

Chapter Three

The big black duck ate the Duck Food box.

afraid

Fred's head looks
like a Duck Food box.

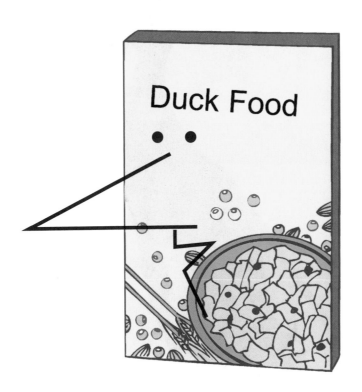

The big black duck wasn't a duck.
It was a big sign.

The ducks laughed.

Quack means Ha! Ha!

The ducks looked around.

a very happy duck